Cock~a~Moo~ Moo

For Tony, Amelia, Alexander and Theo – J.D-C.

To my auntie, Madeleine – you're a star! – A.B.

First published 2001 by Macmillan Children's Books
This edition published 2002 by Macmillan Children's Books
a division of Macmillan Publishers Limited
20 New Wharf Road, London N1 9RR
Basingstoke and Oxford
Associated companies throughout the world
www.panmacmillan.com

ISBN 978-1-5098-0147-3

Text copyright © Juliet Dallas-Conté 2001
Illustrations copyright © Alison Bartlett 2001
Moral rights asserted.

1 3 5 7 9 8 6 4 2

A CIP catalogue record for this book is available from the British Library.

Printed in China

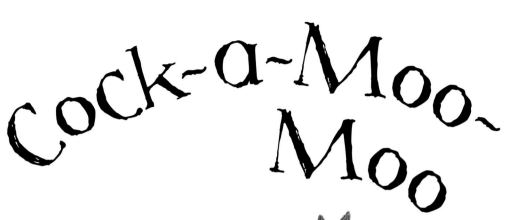

by Juliet Dallas-Conté

illustrated by Alison Bartlett

MACMILLAN
CHILDREN'S BOOKS

Poor Cockerel had forgotten how to crow.

When the sun came up in the morning, he took a deep breath and shouted . . .

"COCK-A-MOO-MOO!"

"That's not right!"
said the cows.
"Only cows go moo."

So he tried again.

"COCK-A-

QUACK-QUACK!"

"That's not right!" said the ducks.
"Only ducks go quack."

So he tried again.

"COCK-A-BAA-BAA!"

"That's not right!" said the sheep.
"Only sheep go baa."

"Silly Cockerel!"
said the chickens.
"You're getting it all wrong."

Cockerel was very unhappy. "I'm never going to crow again," he said.

But that night, when all the animals were asleep, Cockerel heard a noise.

Someone was sniffing . . .
and rustling . . . and sneaking
into the hen house! It was a . . .

FOX!

"COCK-A-MOO-MOO!"

shouted Cockerel.

"COCK-A-QUACK-QUACK!

COCK-A-OINK-OINK!

COCK-A-BAA-BAA!"

All the animals woke up!

They came running and chased the fox away.

"We're saved," clucked the chickens.
"You're a hero!" cried all the animals.
Cockerel was so happy.

"COCK-A-DOODLE-DOO!"

he crowed.

And he never got it wrong again.

ALSO PUBLISHED BY MACMILLAN:

Sammy's Surprise Deliveries
by Rachael Mortimer
illustrated by Janet Samuel

Dinosaur Starts School
by Pamela Duncan Edwards
illustrated by Deborah Allwright

MACMILLAN CHILDREN'S BOOKS